This book belongs to:

_____

For all the friends of CARL

Carl

And the Mysterious Nibbler

Knock! Knock!
"Hello, hello, is anyone home?" called an anxious voice outside the Munk front door.

Carl and Suzy, who were playing checkers, stopped their game.

Mrs. Munk opened the front door. There stood Willie Mouse, glasses askew with grass and sticks stuck to his fur. "Hi, Mrs. Munk," he said breathlessly. "Ran all the way. . . need to . . . talk to Carl."

Outside on his favorite log Carl heard Willie say . . .

"heard two guides . . . talking . . . big mystery . . . up at the Museum."

"I better go see if anyone needs help," said Carl, and he hurried into his bedroom and grabbed his backpack.

"Going up the Museum,"
Carl called to his Mom.

"I'll be back for
dinner." And he hurried
out the front door.

Carl stopped and thanked Willie. "I'll tell you what
I found out later," he said, and up the path he ran.

Once inside the Museum, Carl knew something was very wrong. Everyone was peering down the staff hall. Out the open door . . .

. . . of the Archive Room came the unhappy voices of the Chief Preparator and the Curator of Art. Carl went across the hall to see. . .

. . . Ron, the Chief Preparator, looking down at a drawing of a white-tailed deer.

"Something has made a mess of this Bob Kuhn sketch," he said sadly.

"Oh, dear, what is doing this?" wailed the Curator of Art, Dr. Harris, as he peered through a large hole on a Kuhn drawing of a black bear.

After the men left the Archive Room, Carl climbed up on the table to see the sketches. From his backpack, he took a ruler, a magnifying glass . . .

. . . a note pad and a pencil. Carl took careful measurements and made many notes about what he observed.

"Good clues," hc thought. "I hope they help solve this mystery."

That night after dinner,
Carl dried the dishes . . .

Took mystery books
from his book case . . .

And read way past his bedtime,
looking for answers.

Breakfast was some delicious sunflower seeds and thistle tea . . .

. . . then Carl used his computer for more help . . .

And sat on his favorite log thinking.

After lunch, Carl led an art tour at the Museum. "Please stay together," he reminded the group.

His tour crowded close to study
Bob Kuhn's "Pas de Deux."

"This famous wildlife artist also
did wonderful sketches," said Carl.

As Carl finished the tour and
was saying goodbye to his group,
he realized one of the group
members was missing. But who?

He raced back to the Clymer Studio
where Carl remembered everyone had
been together . . . no one there.

Carl dashed into the Bison Gallery and hopped
up on a bench . . . no missing guest there.

Down the staff hall Carl ran.
He looked in every corner of
each office . . . no luck!

As he moved towards the Archive Room,
Carl saw the tip of a tail just disappearing
under the door.

Carl tried to squeeze under the door.
He didn't fit. "Who's there?" he called.
Hearing no answer, Carl decided to
head home for dinner.

The next morning Carl went to Willie Mouse's house to share his news.

The two friends agreed to set a trap to catch the culprit. "I want to solve this mystery," said Carl. "I know what did this, but not who."

Late that afternoon, Carl and Willie slipped into the Archive Room and hid themselves.

They waited . . .
and waited . . .
and waited . . .
until they heard soft noises and then . . . Something was on the table!

On came the light.

"Stop!"

shouted Carl and Willie. There on the table, caught in the glare of the light . . .

. . . stood the thin, nervous mouse from Carl's afternoon tour group about to take a **bite** out of a Bob Kuhn sketch!!

"Uncle Twitch! How could you?" cried Willie Mouse. "These treasured drawings are from one of the world's greatest wildlife artists."

"He's your uncle?" asked Carl.

"Yes," said Willie sadly.

"They taste so delicious," whined Uncle Twitch.

"Bob Kuhn's sketches aren't for eating, Uncle Twitch!" exclaimed Willie.

"Sir, you are going to write an apology and NEVER do this again," said Carl.

The following morning when the Curator of Art and
the Chief Preparator came into the Archive Room . . .

... they found a small,
handwritten note that said . .

Ron, Chief Preparator, showed the Museum staff the note from Uncle Twitch. "Carl solved the mystery for us. What a special fellow he is!"

"Does Carl need a new badge?" asked Bob, the Security Guard.

"Hmmm," said Dr. Harris, "We should give him a new name. Let's call him . . .

"Detective Carl!"

Carl's Glossary

apology......words that show you are sorry for something you did or said.

Archive Room......a special room in the Museum where objects in the Collection are stored and carefully preserved.

askew......something that looks crooked or off-center.

Chief Preparator......the person who puts up and takes down the Museum's artwork when it goes on exhibit. Preparators also do "behind the scenes" work of packing and unpacking art and storing it safely and securely.

clue......a piece of information that helps you solve a mystery.

collection......a group of similar things. All gathered on purpose, as in an art collection.

...AND UNCLE TWITCH?

WELL, HE LEARNED HIS
LESSON AND NOW COLLECTS
HIS OWN SEEDS, NUTS AND
CHEESE.

IN FACT, HE NOW
WORKS AT THE MUSEUM...

culprit......a person (or animal) who is guilty of doing something wrong.

Curator of Art......the person who selects art for an exhibit and writes about it in the form of labels, articles, and books. The Curator also helps pick new art for the Museum's Collection.

guide......a person who shows a group around the Museum, telling them about the art.

mystery......something that is hard to understand or explain.

nibbler......something that eats by taking small bites.

"Pas de Deux"......A famous painting by Bob Kuhn of a leaping rabbit and a fox. The French words mean "a dance for two."

peer......to look at something closely and searchingly.

public......all the people in the community.

sketch......a quick, rough drawing usually done in pencil or pen.

tour......a guided walk around the Museum to see and learn about the art.

trap......anything that can be used to catch someone or something.

treasure......valuable things like gold, silver, money, art, or other things that have been collected or hidden.

wail......a long cry of pain or sadness.

CARL and the Mysterious Nibbler
Text copyright © 2011 by Lynn Estes Friess,
Mariposa Ranch Press
Illustrations copyright © 2011 by John Potter

Second Printing February 2016

ISBN-13: 978-0-615-50529-9

Mariposa Ranch Press
P.O.Box 9790
Jackson, Wyoming 83002
(307)- 733-2647
www.mariposaranchpress.com

ILLUSTRATED BY John Potter
WRITTEN BY Lynn Estes Friess
DESIGNED BY Carole Thickstun, www.ormsbythickstun.com
PRINTED RESPONSIBLY BY Paragon Press, Salt Lake City, UT
This publication was printed using Ecotech vegetable based inks
on Sterling Ultra Matte manufactured by NewPage U.S.A. The
fiber was sourced from well managed forests and contains 10%
post consumer waste.

Library of Congress Cataloging pending

NATIONAL MUSEUM
of WILDLIFE ART

Proceeds from this book go to help sponsor programs for
children, adults, exhibits, and to provide operating support
for the National Museum of Wildlife Art, Jackson, Wyoming.
Visit their site at www.wildlifeart.org.

A special thanks to Jane Lavino, Sugden Family Curator of
Education, National Museum of Wildlife Art

...GUARDING
THE
BOB KUHN
DRAWINGS!

Signed,
THE AUTHOR

THE END

almost...